KATIE KAZOO, SWITCHEROO

Flower Power

by Nancy Krulik • illustrated by John & Wendy

Grosset & Dunlap

For those who help kids
learn to love to learn—N.K.

For Mary—pop princess with awesome
powers!—J&W

GROSSET & DUNLAP
Published by the Penguin Group
Penguin Group (USA) Inc., 375 Hudson Street,
New York, New York 10014, U.S.A.
Penguin Group (Canada), 90 Eglinton Avenue East, Suite 700,
Toronto, Ontario, Canada M4P 2Y3
(a division of Pearson Penguin Canada Inc.)
Penguin Books Ltd, 80 Strand, London WC2R 0RL, England
Penguin Ireland, 25 St Stephen's Green, Dublin 2, Ireland
(a division of Penguin Books Ltd)
Penguin Group (Australia), 250 Camberwell Road, Camberwell,
Victoria 3124, Australia
(a division of Pearson Australia Group Pty Ltd)
Penguin Books India Pvt Ltd, 11 Community Centre, Panchsheel Park,
New Delhi - 110 017, India
Penguin Group (NZ), 67 Apollo Drive, Rosedale, North Shore 0745, Auckland,
New Zealand (a division of Pearson New Zealand Ltd.)
Penguin Books (South Africa) (Pty) Ltd, 24 Sturdee Avenue, Rosebank,
Johannesburg 2196, South Africa

Penguin Books Ltd, Registered Offices:
80 Strand, London WC2R 0RL, England

Library of Congress Control Number: 2007010705

ISBN 978-0-448-44674-5   10 9 8 7 6

Chapter 1

The minute Katie Carew walked into her fourth-grade classroom, she began giggling. Her teacher, Mr. Guthrie, looked so funny. He was wearing bright green pants and a green turtleneck shirt. A circle of white construction-paper petals framed his face. He looked like a giant daisy.

The Mr. G.-daisy fit right in with the 4A classroom. Paper flowers hung from the classroom ceiling. Plastic flowers were strewn around the floor. And there was a daisy chain around Slinky the snake's cage.

"Let me guess; we're learning about flowers today," George Brennan, one of Katie's

classmates, predicted as he plopped down in his beanbag chair.

"What makes you say that?" Emma Weber joked, looking at a bouquet of plastic roses on a windowsill.

"Just a wild guess," George laughed, picking up a pink and white tissue-paper carnation.

"A wild*flower* guess," Kadeem Carter added.

"That's right, dudes. Our next learning adventure is the life cycle of a flower," Mr. G. said. "So hurry up and start decorating your beanbags, because I have a huge surprise for you."

"What's the surprise?" Mandy Banks asked excitedly.

"It wouldn't be a surprise if he told us," Kevin Camilleri reminded her.

Katie grinned as she taped purple and yellow paper pansies to her beanbag chair. She loved decorating her beanbag. She got to do it every time the class learned about something new. All of the kids in class 4A sat in beanbags. Mr. G. thought kids learned better when they were comfortable. Katie and her classmates totally agreed.

Katie's class did a lot of unusual things in fourth grade. There was the time they were studying birds, and Mr. G. made them all dig worms out of the mud and eat them. (Luckily, they were just gummy worms buried in chocolate pudding!)

And who could forget when Mr. G. had dressed like Abraham Lincoln for Presidents' Day?

Or the way he had turned the kids into fish (or at least had them *pretend* to be fish) when they were studying ocean life?

Now, today, Katie's teacher was dressed like a giant daisy and standing in the middle of what looked more like a garden than a classroom. And there was still another giant surprise to come! Mr. G. was definitely the greatest teacher in the world!

× × ×

"Okay, dudes, gather round," Mr. G. said once everyone finished decorating their beanbags.

The kids hurried to the front of the room where Mr. G. removed some clay pots and a bag of dirt from the closet.

"We're planting flowers," Kevin guessed. He sounded kind of disappointed.

Katie knew how he felt. Planting flowers

was a really normal classroom activity. Usually Mr. G.'s projects were more interesting than that.

Mr. G. was holding several white envelopes. One by one, he handed them out to the kids. "There are seeds inside each envelope," Mr. G. explained. "Flower seeds."

"What kind of flower will I grow?" Katie asked Mr. G. The seed packet Mr. G. handed her had no name or picture on it.

"That's for me to know and you to find out," he told her.

"You mean, I'll find out when it pops up out of the dirt?" Katie asked.

Mr. G. shook his head. "You'll find out sooner than that. You have something else besides the seeds. Inside each of your envelopes is a list of clues about the flower you will be growing. It's your job to figure out from the clues what kind of flower seeds you have."

Katie opened her packet and took out a piece of paper. She read what was written on it.

The ancient Aztec people thought this flower was magical.

Today it is used in Africa and India to color foods such as butter and cheese.

This is an unusually tough flower. It can grow in mild to cool temperatures as long as it is in sunlight.

Can you figure out what your mystery flower is?

Katie smiled broadly. A mystery flower. Now *that* was very, very Mr. G.!

Chapter 2

"Hi, Katie," Jeremy Fox said as he placed his tray down next to hers in the school cafeteria later that day.

"Hi!" Katie replied happily. She was so glad to see Jeremy. He and Katie's other best friend, Suzanne Lock, were in Ms. Sweet's fourth-grade class. Katie only got to see them during lunch and recess. "Where's everyone else?" she asked.

"In the bathroom," Jeremy replied as he took a huge bite of his tuna hero.

"They all had to go at the same time?" Katie asked, amazed.

Jeremy laughed and shook his head. "We

were planting seeds, so Ms. Sweet made us wash our hands before lunch. I got to the boys' room first."

Katie nodded. No surprise there. Jeremy was the fastest runner in the fourth grade. A moment later, most of the other kids in class 4B arrived in the cafeteria. Naturally, Suzanne sat on the other side of Katie and pretty much ignored Jeremy. That was nothing new. Katie's two best friends weren't really friends with each other. And Suzanne hated it when Jeremy and Katie spent time alone together.

"Can you believe Miriam Chan?" Suzanne said, staring in Miriam's direction. "She is *so* looking for attention."

"What are you talking about?" Katie said.

"Did you see what she's having for lunch?" Suzanne asked her.

Katie looked. Miriam was drinking something from a blue container.

"It's a vitamin shake," Jeremy told the girls. "I drink a lot of them during soccer season. They're really healthy."

"What's the big deal?" Katie asked Suzanne.

"She's only drinking the shake so everyone will see her new braces," Suzanne explained. "She says her mouth hurts so much, she can't eat regular food."

"It probably does," Jeremy said. "She's got a lot of wires in there."

"Miriam got braces? Cool!" Katie exclaimed. "I want to see."

"That's what I mean," Suzanne harrumphed. "It's for attention."

"Braces are for straightening teeth," Jeremy told her. "There are plenty of other ways to get attention. *You* should know."

Katie knew exactly what Jeremy meant. Suzanne hated when anyone besides her was in the spotlight.

And right now, Miriam was definitely the center of attention. The kids were gathered around her, staring at her teeth. Katie went over to join them. "I heard you got braces, Miriam," she said.

"Yes, yesterday," Miriam replied. She sounded kind of uncomfortable.

"Do they hurt a lot?" Katie asked her.

Miriam nodded. "But I put some wax on the wires. The orthodontist says they will feel better in a day or two."

"What color wires did you pick?" Emma W. asked Miriam.

"Red and pink," Miriam said, smiling so everyone could see the brightly colored wires that lined her braces. "But I can change them next month. They have lots of cool colors to choose from. Blue, green, yellow, even glow-in-the-dark."

"*That* would be really cool for sleepovers," Jessica Haynes suggested.

"I think it would be gross," Suzanne remarked from her seat a few feet away. "Braces are not cool. They're ugly."

Miriam looked like she was about to cry.

"Suzanne!" Katie scolded. "That's not nice."

But Suzanne ignored Katie. "I'm glad I have such straight, white teeth," she continued. "They'll be perfect for when I'm in a toothpaste ad."

"When are you going to do that?" Jessica asked.

"I don't know," Suzanne replied. "But I'm sure I will someday. My teeth are perfect."

"Miriam's teeth are going to be perfect, too," Katie told Suzanne. "As soon as her braces come off." She smiled at Miriam, hoping she had made her feel better.

Miriam smiled back, a little.

"I think they make you look kind of grown-up," Emma W. told her. "Like an almost teenager."

"Oh, no!" Suzanne yelped. Her juice fell to the floor, catching everyone's attention. Katie turned around just in time to see Suzanne leaping out of the way.

"Oops!" Suzanne exclaimed. "What a mess."

Katie sighed. She had a feeling Suzanne had done that on purpose, just to get the focus back on her.

"Katie, could you help me clean this up?" Suzanne asked, grabbing a pile of napkins from her tray.

"Um . . . sure," Katie said. She frowned slightly. She couldn't just let her best friend stand there in a puddle of red fruit punch, could she?

It didn't take very long for Katie and Suzanne to clean up the mess. A few minutes later, things were back to normal. Katie was seated between Jeremy and Suzanne. And once again, Suzanne was the center of attention.

"I got geranium seeds to plant," she boasted. "They are such beautiful flowers. They're going to be bright red."

"I got impatiens," Jeremy said. "I'm going to give them to my mother to plant in our garden when they're big enough." He turned to Katie. "What flower did you plant?"

"I don't know," Katie told him.

"You're not planting seeds?" Suzanne

asked. "What a bummer. We had a lot of fun doing that in *our* class."

"We will be planting seeds," Katie assured her. "It's just that I don't know what flowers are going to come up."

"Why not?" Jeremy asked curiously.

"We all got mystery flowers," Katie explained. "We have to use the clues Mr. G. gave us to find out what we're growing. After we solve the mystery, we'll get to plant our seeds."

"It's fun," George said, looking up from the disgusting mush of tuna, Jell-O, and fruit punch he'd been creating on his tray. He pulled a slip of paper from his pocket. "'This flower was used by native Americans for food and oil,'" he read aloud. "'Some farmers use it to feed their animals. It's the national flower of Russia.'"

"I wonder what that could be," Jeremy said.

"My flower smells very sweet," Kevin chimed in. "It's used for decoration and it comes in a lot of colors. Some of them are even striped!"

"Mystery flowers," Jeremy remarked. "Wow. Mr. G. sure has a lot of cool ideas."

"Oh, give me a break!" Suzanne exclaimed. "It's a *dumb* idea."

"No it's not," Katie said. "I love solving mysteries."

Suzanne sighed. "I can't stand this place anymore. Everyone's talking about dumb things like braces and mystery flowers. I wish I went to a school where people cared about *important things*, like fashion and makeup."

"You do not!" Katie exclaimed suddenly. "You do not wish that at all!"

"Whoa, Katie Kazoo, calm down," George said, using the way-cool nickname he'd given her. "Suzanne's just being Suzanne. It's no big deal."

But Katie knew that wasn't true. Wishes were a very big deal. And only Katie knew why.

Chapter 3

Wishes were dangerous.

Katie had learned that lesson after one
really bad day back in third grade. That day,
after dropping the ball, she lost the football
game for her team. Then mud got all over her
favorite pants. Worst of all, she'd let out a
giant burp in front of the whole class. Talk
about embarrassing!

That night, Katie had wished that she
could be anyone but herself. There must have
been a shooting star flying overhead, because
the next day the magic wind came.

The magic wind was a big tornado that
swirled only around Katie. It was so powerful

that it could turn her into somebody else! The first time the magic wind came, it turned Katie into Speedy, class 3A's hamster. She'd spent the whole morning running round and round on a hamster wheel. And when she finally escaped from her cage, she'd wound up inside George's stinky sneaker. YUCK!

Since then, the magic wind had been back again and again. One time it turned her into Mr. Starkey, the school music teacher. The band sounded really terrible when Katie was the conductor!

And then there was the time Katie had turned into Dr. Sang, her dentist, at the very moment Emma W.'s little brother Matthew was having his first checkup. Matthew was scared to begin with. But once Katie made a mess of things, little Matthew vowed he would never, *ever*, open his mouth for a dentist again!

That was the worst thing about the magic wind. Every time it came, the person Katie turned into landed in big trouble. Then it was up to Katie to make things all right again. That wasn't always so easy. Katie ended up having a checkup herself, just to show Matthew that going to the dentist wasn't so bad!

That was why Katie didn't make wishes anymore. They caused too many problems if they came true.

Of course, Katie couldn't tell her friends about her switcheroos. They wouldn't believe her even if she did. Katie wouldn't believe it either—if it didn't keep happening to her.

Right now all of her friends were looking at her as though she were nuts. Not that she blamed them. She had gone a little crazy when Suzanne made that wish.

"I . . . uh . . . I just meant that I would be really sad if you went to a different school," Katie told Suzanne.

"Of course you would," Suzanne said. "But don't worry. I'll be going to school with you for a long, long time."

"Oh, man," George moaned. He poured more fruit punch into the yucky mixture on his tray. "I've definitely lost my appetite."

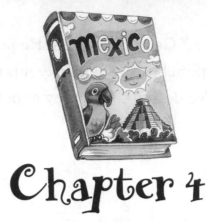

Chapter 4

Okay, so if my flower is used to color butter, it must be yellow, Katie thought to herself as she sat in the school library later that afternoon.

"How's it going, Katie?" Ms. Folio, the school librarian, asked.

"I'm trying to guess what my mystery flower is," Katie told her. "So far, all I know is it's a yellow flower that the Aztecs thought had magic power."

"The ancient Aztecs lived in Mexico," Ms. Folio told Katie. "Let's find a book about the history of Mexico. Maybe your flower is mentioned."

"I got it!" George shouted suddenly from his seat at one of the library computers. "My flower is a sunflower!"

"Good detective work, George," Mr. G. congratulated him. "Now see if you can find some more interesting facts about sunflowers."

"It says here they grow eight to twelve feet tall," George replied.

Now that George knew what flower he had, Katie was even more excited to discover what kind of seeds where in *her* packet. She searched through a book on the Aztecs for some clue about what her flower might be. At last she spotted something in a chapter called "Magic and Medicine." The answer was right there! *The yellow marigold was once believed to contain magic pain-relieving powers. Today the flower is used to calm the pain and swelling of bee stings.*

"My mystery flower is a marigold!" she exclaimed. "Is that right, Mr. G.?"

Mr. G. grinned. "Good for you, Katie

Kazoo," he rhymed. "You've solved the mystery."

Katie smiled proudly back at him. She felt like a real detective who had just solved a big case.

Soon all of the detectives in class 4A had solved their mysteries. Everyone knew just what flowers would be popping their heads out of the dirt. Katie couldn't wait to see all the flowers—especially her marigolds.

But she would have to wait. According to a book on flowers Ms. Folio had found for her, marigold sprouts didn't pop up until a week after the seeds were planted. It would be eight whole weeks before the yellow flowers bloomed.

Brrriiiinnnng!

Just then, the school bell rang. It was the end of the day.

"Okay, detective dudes, pack up. It's time to go home!" Mr. G. told them.

Katie grinned. Mr. G. had them bring their

backpacks and coats to the library. Now they could leave school without stopping back in the classroom. In a flash, the kids in class 4A were heading outside.

"That was so much fun!" Katie exclaimed happily as she and Emma W. walked down the hallway together.

"I can't wait to read more about daisies," Emma W. replied. "They're my mystery flower."

"And I am going to learn more about marigo—" Katie stopped midsentence. "Oops. I left one of my books in the library."

"Go back and get it," Emma said. "I'll wait for you."

Katie ran back to the library. When she got there, it was completely empty—except for Mr. G. and Ms. Folio. They were by Ms. Folio's desk in back. Whatever they were talking about must have been very important. They didn't even notice that Katie had come in.

Katie knew it was wrong to eavesdrop.

But she couldn't help herself. She'd always wondered what teachers talked about when kids weren't around.

"So when are you going to do it?" Katie heard Ms. Folio ask.

"In about an hour," Mr. G. replied. "It's sure going to feel weird having short hair. I've had this ponytail since college."

"Change is good," Ms. Folio told him.

"I guess," Mr. G. agreed. "Oh, wow. Look at the time. I've got to go. I need to pick up my suit before I go to the barber."

And with that, Mr. G. turned and headed for the door. He stopped when he spotted Katie. "Hi, Katie," he said cheerfully.

Did he know she'd been listening? "Uh . . . hi," she answered. "I . . . um . . . forgot my book."

"Ms. Folio's still here. It was very responsible of you to come back and get it," Mr. G. told her. "I'll see you tomorrow," he added as he breezed past her and out the door, his long ponytail flopping up and down behind him.

Katie frowned. Mr. G. without a ponytail? How weird would that be?

Chapter 5

"You guys are never gonna believe this!" Katie shouted as she raced over to where her friends were standing outside school.

"What?" Emma W. asked.

"Mr. G. is cutting off his ponytail!" Katie exclaimed.

That sure got everyone's attention.

"No way!" George said.

"Way," Katie assured him.

"How would *you* know something like that?" Suzanne demanded.

Katie sighed. Suzanne could sound so mean when someone else found out something before she did.

"I heard Mr. G. tell Ms. Folio that he was going to the barbershop," she told Suzanne. "So I know it's the truth."

"Whoa, Mr. G. with short hair," Kevin said. "That would make him look . . ."

"Like a normal teacher," Suzanne finished his sentence.

"Mr. G. could never be normal," George  told Suzanne.

"Yeah, he's special," Emma W. agreed.

Suzanne rolled her eyes. "I don't see what's so special about your teacher. I like Ms. Sweet much better."

"He would just have short hair," Kevin insisted.

"But he'd still be Mr. G. He'd still be wearing the same clothes and . . ."

"No he won't," Katie interrupted him. "He said something about having to pick up a suit, too."

"A suit?" Jeremy repeated. "But Mr. G. never wears a suit. Only people who work in offices wear those."

Suddenly a smile appeared on Suzanne's face. "Maybe that's what Mr. G. is going to do," she said.

"What?" Katie asked her.

"Work in an office," Suzanne told her. "Maybe Mr. G. is looking for a new job."

"Mr. G. would never do that," George insisted.

Suzanne shrugged. "I'm just saying it's possible. Maybe he's got a job interview coming up and he wants to look all businesslike for it."

"It is not possible!" George insisted. "Mr. G. isn't going anywhere. He's our teacher and he's going to stay right here."

Suddenly Katie felt horrible. Imagining fourth grade without Mr. G. was just too awful.

Chapter 6

"Okay, dudes, follow the directions for planting your seeds carefully," Mr. G. said as the kids in class 4A filled their flowerpots with dirt early the next morning.

Katie placed the seeds a few inches apart and covered them with a thin layer of soil just as the instructions in the packet told her to. She wanted to make sure her marigold seeds grew up to be big, beautiful, yellow flowers.

But it was hard to pay attention to what she was doing. Katie's eyes kept drifting over to Mr. G. He seemed so different without his long ponytail. He looked so . . . so . . . *normal.*

"Don't you like my new haircut?" was all he'd say.

"Okay, you guys," Mr. G. said a moment later. "When everyone's seeds are planted, we're going to go outside and do some yoga. We can do poses that imitate the way seeds open up to the sun."

Katie smiled. With or without his ponytail, Mr. G. was still Mr. G.

"Oh, and before I forget," Mr. G. continued, "you are going to have a substitute teacher tomorrow. I have an appointment I have to keep."

Katie, Emma W., George, and Kevin all looked at each other nervously. An appointment? Like an *interview* appointment for another job?

"I expect you all to be as well behaved for the new teacher as you are for me," Mr. G. told the kids.

"*New* teacher?" Katie asked him nervously.

"The substitute teacher," Mr. G. explained.

"But the substitute's only coming tomorrow?" Katie asked, making sure. "You'll be back after that, right?"

"That's the plan," he said.

Katie frowned. That didn't sound too convincing. She wanted Mr. G. to promise to come back to school the day after tomorrow and never leave again.

× × ×

"Check out Miriam *now*," Suzanne groaned as she, Katie, Emma W., Mandy, George, and Kevin all stood outside the school building after school.

"She looks perfectly normal to me," Emma W. said.

"It's her hair," Suzanne urged.

The kids all looked over at Miriam. Her hair looked like it always did. Long, black, and straight. Today she was wearing pigtails.

"What are you talking about, Suzanne?" Mandy asked. "What's wrong with pigtails?"

"She's wearing pink and red ribbons,"

Suzanne pointed out. "She's just doing that so her hair matches the wires in her braces."

"Oh, cool," Emma W. said.

"No it's not," Suzanne insisted. "Nothing is going to make those braces look cool. Miriam should just give it up. Don't you think so, Katie?"

But Katie didn't answer. She hadn't really been listening to Suzanne.

"Katie?" Suzanne repeated louder.

"What? Oh sorry," Katie said, realizing she hadn't been paying attention. "I was thinking about something else."

"What?" Suzanne asked in a voice that made it sound like nothing could be more important than anything she said.

But something was more important. *Much* more.

"She's worrying about Mr. G.," Kevin explained. "We all are."

"What about him?" Suzanne said. "So what if he doesn't have his ponytail."

"It's not just that," Katie told her. "He told us today that he's going to be absent tomorrow. He has an appointment."

Suzanne smiled triumphantly. "I knew it! He's looking for another job!"

Katie couldn't believe Suzanne looked so happy about being right. Especially when all her friends were so miserable.

"We have to stop him," Emma W. insisted. "We have to make sure Mr. G. stays."

"But how can we do that?" Katie asked.

George thought for a minute. "Tomorrow, when the substitute comes, we have to really act up!" he exclaimed suddenly.

"What good would that do?" Mandy asked him.

"If the principal thinks Mr. G. is the only teacher who can make us behave, he'll beg him to stay," George explained. "Maybe he'll give him a big raise so Mr. G. won't want a new job."

"I don't think that's such a great idea," Emma W. said.

"Yeah, Mr. G asked us to be well behaved," Katie added.

"But if we behave, he won't be our teacher anymore," George insisted.

"You really think so?" Katie didn't like the idea of giving a teacher a hard time. But the kids could not let Mr. G. leave. No way! And George's plan was the only one they had at the moment.

"Okay, so let's go home and e-mail the rest of 4A and tell them what we're going to do," George said. "Everyone has to be really bad tomorrow."

"That will never work," Suzanne said. "Face it. Mr. G. is on his way out."

"Stop it, Suzanne!" Katie scolded her angrily. "George's plan *will* work! It has to."

Chapter 7

MR. GOODSTEIN

Katie frowned as she watched the substitute teacher write his name across the blackboard. She had been in her classroom only five minutes, and already things with Mr. Goodstein were not very "good."

The substitute hadn't been happy that there were no desks for class 4A. He had asked the kids to arrange their beanbag chairs in neat rows on the floor. That made 4A almost look like a normal classroom. Worse yet, Katie was sitting behind Mandy. Mandy was very tall, which made it difficult for Katie to see the board.

"Please take out your science notebooks," Mr. Goodstein told the class. "We are going to learn the vocabulary for the parts of the plant." He picked up a piece of chalk and began to write. "The basic parts of a plant are the roots, stems, leaves . . ."

Bam. Just then, George dropped his notebook—accidentally on purpose—on the floor.

Bam. Kevin dropped his notebook on the floor, too.

The trouble had begun.

Bam. Katie slammed her notebook hard on the floor. It felt so weird to misbehave on purpose. Katie was not at all sure she liked it.

Bam. Bam. Andrew and Emma Stavros dropped their notebooks.

Bam. Bam. Bam. Kadeem, Mandy, and Emma W. all dropped theirs as well.

"What is going on here?" Mr. Goodstein demanded.

"Sorry," George said with a mischievous

grin. "We're kind of a clumsy class."

"I can see that," Mr. Goodstein replied with a sigh. "Pick up your notebooks and let's get back to work."

The kids did as they were told. They picked up the books, opened to a clean page and . . .

"*Cough, cough.*" Kevin suddenly started coughing wildly.

"*Cough, cough, cough,*" George chimed in, coughing even harder.

That made Kadeem let out his own long, loud chain of coughs. "*Cough, cough, cough, COUGH!*"

"*Cough, cough,*" Andrew joined in. He was followed by Andrew, Mandy, the two Emmas, and Katie.

"*Cough, cough, cough, cough, cough . . .*"

"Stop it! Stop it right now!" Mr. Goodstein bellowed.

"*Cough . . . cough . . .*" The kids kept coughing.

"I think we all need some water," George

said. "Can we go to the water fountain? *Cough,*
cough . . ."

Mr. Goodstein sighed. "Nothing will get
done until you do, I suppose," he said angrily.
"Go into the hallway, stand in line, and get your
water. And be quick about it."

Katie and her classmates jumped up from
their seats and quickly ran to the fountain. A
few moments later, they were all back in their
neatly arranged beanbag chairs.

Katie glanced over at George. He looked
weird. His cheeks were all puffy. Was he sick?

Nope. George wasn't sick. It was all a trick. A
moment later he pursed his lips and . . . *whoosh!*
He spit a stream of water from his mouth.

"Look at George, he's a water fountain!"
Kevin screamed excitedly. "That's so cool,
George!"

Mr. Goodstein did not agree. "You, you there.
The boy with the dribble of water on his shirt.
Go out into the hall. Stay there until you can
behave."

Katie knew George wasn't all that upset to be sent out. It used to happen to him all the time last year. Their strict third-grade teacher, Mrs. Derkman (or Mrs. *Jerk*man as George liked to call her), was always sending him into the hall for misbehaving. Of course, now, with Mr. G. for a teacher, George was better behaved. Katie figured that was because he was happier.

But Katie bet George would be back to his old self if Mr. Goodstein—who was more like Mr. *Bad*stein—went from substitute teacher to permanent teacher. That would be *so* not good!

× × ×

After a tiring morning of coughing, book dropping, and water spitting, the kids in class 1A had a well deserved lunch and recess. And by the time they returned to the classroom, they were ready to get back to Operation Keep Mr. G.

"Now, let's talk about the flower of the plant," Mr. Goodstein said as the kids took their seats.

"Speaking of flowers," George began. "Do you guys know what the bee said to the rose?"

"What?" Mandy asked him.

"Hi, bud!" George answered, chuckling.

The class all laughed with him. Mr. Goodstein did not join in. "Excuse me, but we are discussing science and . . ."

"Do you know what flower is the happiest?" Kadeem interrupted the substitute teacher.

"Which one?" Emma S. asked.

"The *glad*iola!" Kadeem replied.

The class all laughed again.

"It's a flower joke-off!" Kevin exclaimed. "Awesome."

"Why do gardeners hate weeds?" George shouted.

"Why?" Andrew asked.

"Because if you give them one inch, they'll take the whole yard!" George joked.

"If April showers bring May flowers, what do May flowers bring?" Kadeem asked the class.

"What?" Emma W. replied.

"Pilgrims!" Kadeem shouted. "Get it, Mayflower? Pilgrims?"

The kids all laughed really hard at that one.

"That's enough!" Mr. Goodstein shouted angrily. "Stop the clowning around. This is school. And school is serious business."

The kids all stopped laughing immediately. All except Katie, that is. She wasn't trying to be bad. It was just that that last joke had been so funny. She couldn't stop laughing.

"You—the girl with the red hair!" Mr. Goodstein bellowed. He pointed right at Katie. "Out, now!"

What! Katie's heart skipped a beat. She had never been sent out of a classroom before. She blinked a few times so the tears wouldn't come. Then she stood up and walked quietly out of the classroom.

This is all to keep Mr. G., she reminded herself.

As the door closed behind her, Katie stood there, alone in the hallway. It was a horrible feeling. She didn't know how George could stand it.

Suddenly Katie heard loud footsteps coming down the hall. She turned and came face-to-face with Mr. Kane, the school principal.

"Katie, what are you doing out here?" he asked her.

Katie gulped. "I . . . um . . . some kids were telling jokes, and I was laughing and . . ."

Just then, a chorus of dropping notebooks could be heard coming from the classroom.

"What is going on?" Mr. Kane demanded.

"It's the new substitute," Katie said. "He doesn't know how to control us. Not the way Mr. G. does. *He's* the best teacher. Everyone is

always well behaved for *him*. But today, with Mr. Goodstein, everyone is being bad."

"Well, that's going to stop right now!" Mr. Kane said as he opened the door and stormed into the room.

Katie smiled. She had let Mr. Kane know what a great teacher Mr. G. was. The principal would never let him leave. George's plan was working!

Chapter 8

"It was awesome," Kevin told Jeremy and Suzanne after school that afternoon. "I thought that sub's face was going to explode when George and Kadeem started their joke-off."

"But Katie Kazoo was the real hero," George insisted. He smiled at her. "Because of you, Mr. Kane went into our classroom and saw what was happening."

"Now he knows for sure Mr. G. is the only teacher for class 4A," Kevin added.

"Everything went as planned," George agreed.

"We had some action in our class, too,"

Suzanne boasted. "Miriam hit Manny Gonzalez in the face with a rubber band. She just missed his eye."

"Miriam didn't do it on purpose," Jeremy corrected Suzanne. "The rubber band just popped out of her mouth while she was talking to him."

"I think she did it to remind everyone that she has braces now," Suzanne said. "Like *that's* anything to brag about."

Jeremy rolled his eyes and sighed. "Hey, Katie, you want to come over and play tag this afternoon?" he asked.

"George and I are going to play," Kevin said.

"So are Jessica and I," Suzanne added.

Katie shook her head sadly. She would have liked to play with her friends. But she had something else she had to do. "I've got to go write a hundred-word paper on 'why I should behave in school.' Mr. Kane is making me do it."

"Wow. Bummer," Jeremy said.

"But it's worth it to keep Mr. G.," George reminded her.

I sure hope so, Katie thought to herself as she started walking home alone.

The road to Katie's house was very quiet. No one seemed to be around this afternoon. Suddenly she felt a cool breeze blowing on the back of her neck. Katie shivered. If only she had worn a jacket.

But now Katie noticed that the wind didn't seem to be blowing anywhere else. Not in the trees. Not in the grass. Just on her.

"Oh, no!" Katie shouted. "Go away, magic wind!" She started to run.

It was no use! The magic wind didn't stop blowing. In fact, it blew faster and faster, spinning wildly like a tornado around Katie. She closed her eyes tight to keep from crying.

And then it stopped. Just like that.

Katie Kazoo had turned into someone else. One, two, switcheroo.

But who?

Chapter 9

Katie didn't know where the magic wind had blown her, but wherever she was, it sure smelled clean. Kind of like her house when her mom and dad scrubbed it really, really well before company came.

Slowly, Katie opened her eyes and looked around. The first thing she saw was a long hallway with lots of doors. There was a big, cheerful painting of jungle animals on the wall.

There were other people in the long hallway. Most of them were in green or blue loose-fitting outfits. They had stethoscopes swung around their necks. Katie figured they were doctors and nurses. Was she in some sort of hospital? It sure looked that way.

Okay, so now she knew *where* she was. But she still didn't know *who* she was. Had the magic wind switcherooed her into a doctor? Or a nurse? Katie hoped it hadn't turned her into a patient who was getting a shot. Katie hated needles!

She looked down at her feet. Instead of the light brown cowboy boots she'd worn to school, Katie was now wearing red shoes. Gigantic, rubbery, red shoes. *Clown* shoes! And she had on a polka-dot clown suit with a frilly white collar.

That didn't make any sense at all. What was a clown doing in a hospital?

Just then, a woman walked over toward Katie. "The kids are ready for you, Mr. Guthrie," she said.

Mr. Guthrie? Her teacher? Katie looked around to see if he was standing behind her. But he wasn't. In fact, the only two people

who were standing here were the woman and
Katie.

Katie gulped. The woman was definitely
talking to her. Did that mean that she'd
turned into her teacher . . . in a clown suit?
What was Mr. G. doing dressed as a clown? It
was so weird.

Or maybe not. Mr. G. loved dressing up. So
putting on a clown suit was a really Mr. G.
thing to do.

"The new clown suit is great," the woman continued saying to Katie. "I am so glad it was ready for you in time for this party."

Was *this* the suit Mr. G. had been talking about? Not a businessman suit. A *clown* suit. Was Mr. G. leaving Cherrydale Elementary School to become a clown?

"It was so nice of you to come here on a weekday," the woman continued. "I know you usually do these shows for the kids on Saturdays, but I'm glad you made an exception this one time. Darnell would have been so sad if he left the hospital without saying good-bye to G-Man the Clown."

Okay, now it all was starting to make sense. Mr. G. performed for sick kids. Katie smiled broadly. But coming today was an *exception*! That meant everything would be back to normal by tomorrow. What a relief! Wait until the kids in 4A learned that Mr. G. wasn't leaving school at all. He was just putting on a clown show for some sick kids in the hospital . . .

Gulp! Except Mr. G. wasn't the one putting on the show at all. Katie was. Today Katie was G-Man the Clown! But she didn't know anything about clowning around. That was George's department.

Today, though, *Katie* was going to have to be funny—fast! There was a whole lot of sick kids waiting for her to cheer them up.

"Hello, boys and girls," the woman in the blue outfit said as she and Katie walked into a sunroom. "Look who's here! It's G-Man the Clown!"

"Yeah!" the kids cheered.

Katie stared at them. She wasn't sure what to do. Then she thought about George and Kadeem. They always made people laugh with their jokes. That was it. Katie would tell a joke.

"Hey, do you guys know this one?" she asked. "If April showers bring May flowers, what do pilgrims bring?"

The kids all looked at her strangely.

"Turkey?" one little girl in a wheelchair asked.

"Cranberry sauce?" a small boy with a cast on his leg said.

"You told that one wrong, G-Man the Clown," a skinny boy laughed. "It's supposed to be, 'What do May flowers bring?' Then you answer, 'Pilgrims!'"

Oops. Katie blushed. She'd messed that one up badly. Poor Mr. G. She'd only been here a few minutes and already she was goofing up his clown act.

She thought for a minute. What else besides telling jokes did George do to be funny? Suddenly she spotted a pitcher of water on the table. That was it!

Katie walked over and poured herself a cup of water. Then she took a drink, held the water in her mouth, pursed her lips, and . . .

"Cough! Cough! Cough!" Instead of becoming a water fountain by spitting the water out—Katie took all that water *in*. And

it went down the *wrong* pipe. *"Cough! Cough! Cough!"*

"What's he doing?" a small girl in a wheelchair asked.

"Are you making fun of us, G-Man?" a boy in a blue bathrobe asked. "We can't help being sick."

That made Katie feel terrible. She would never make fun of someone for being sick. Ever!

A tall boy with very, very short hair—so short that you could see his scalp underneath—frowned. "This is the worst going-away party ever!" he sighed.

A nurse came over and wrapped her arm around his shoulder. "Darnell, relax. G-Man the Clown is just getting started. You know he'd never let you down."

Katie sighed. G-Man wouldn't let Darnell down. But Katie sure was. She coughed really hard as the last bit of water went down.

Clank! Just then, a big silver horn fell off of her clown suit. Katie jumped with surprise. Her big clown shoe landed right on the black ball at the end of the horn. *HONK!*

Then the most amazing thing happened. The kids laughed. Hard. They thought Katie had done that on purpose. And they loved it! Katie stepped on the horn again. *Honk!*

Then Katie thought about other funny things a clown might do. *Hmmm.* There was a big plastic flower in her shirt pocket. It would be funny to smell a plastic flower. After all, everyone knew plastic flowers only smelled like . . . well . . . plastic. She picked the big plastic flower from her shirt pocket, bent her head, and . . .

Squirt! A big rush of water hit her in the eye. The kids laughed even harder at the sight of that.

Katie had had no idea that there was water inside the plastic flower. The shock of it threw her off balance. She tripped over one of her huge rubber clown shoes and . . . *Splat!* She landed right on her rear end—and on top of the horn. *Honk!*

And the kids just kept on laughing and laughing!

"G-Man the Clown has a new act," Katie heard one of the nurses say.

"Must be a special show to celebrate Darnell getting well," a doctor replied. "He and Mr. Guthrie are very close."

"Mr. Guthrie is such a great guy," the nurse added. "I hope those kids in his class at school appreciate him."

Oh, we do, Katie wanted to say. But of course, she couldn't. After all, she *was* Mr. G. right now. Or was that G-Man the Clown? Well, either way, she had a show to put on. She hopped up onto her feet and . . . *HONK!*

Chapter 10

"Yay! Hooray!"

Katie could still hear the sick kids cheering for her as she left the sunroom of the hospital and headed down the hallway, toward the lobby. She couldn't wait to get outside.

"Mr. Guthrie, don't you want to change into your regular clothes before you leave?" one of the nurses asked.

Katie gulped. She didn't want to be her teacher when he was in his underwear!

"No. Uh, that's okay. I kind of like this outfit," she said, quickly heading out the door.

It was cool and crisp outside. Katie took a deep breath of the fresh air. It sure felt good to get a whiff of the trees and the grass.

Katie felt really bad for the kids that had to stay in the hospital. They probably would give anything to be out here looking at the flowers and feeling a cool breeze on their necks. That breeze sure did feel good. At least at first . . .

But then that gentle breeze began blowing harder and harder. In a flash, it turned into a wild tornado, blowing just around Katie. The magic wind was back!

The magic wind whirled and swirled wildly. Katie had to hold on to a nearby lamppost just to keep from being blown away.

And then it stopped. Just like that. The magic wind was gone. Katie Kazoo was back.

So was Mr. G. And boy, did he look confused.

"Katie, what are you doing out here in the hospital parking lot?" he asked. Then he paused for a moment. "Come to think of it, what am I doing out here? I'm supposed to be in there doing a show for sick kids."

"I think maybe you already did it," Katie said.

"Did I mess up a joke?" Mr. G. asked her, shaking his head slightly.

Before Mr. G. could ask any more questions, the boy with short, short hair came running over with his mother. Katie remembered that the nurse had called him Darnell. "I forgot to give you this, G-Man," Darnell said. He held out a card he had made.

Mr. G. took the card and opened it up. Katie looked over his shoulder to see what it said.

Thanks, G-Man the Clown. G stands for Great!

Your pal, Darnell

Katie grinned. She knew just what Darnell meant.

"I hope I see you again soon," Darnell said seriously. "Only not in here, you know what I mean?"

Mr. G. grinned. "I know exactly what you

mean. I'm so glad you're well now. Maybe one day *you'll* come back and put on a show for the kids."

"Maybe," Darnell agreed. "But I'll know all the jokes *before* I do my show."

Mr. G. frowned. "I *really* can't believe that happened."

Oh, it did, Katie thought to herself. *And other stuff, too.* But, of course, she didn't say that.

As Darnell walked away, Mr. G.'s cell phone began to ring. "Hello?" he said to the person on the other end.

Katie waited patiently while Mr. G. talked on the phone. He did not look very happy.

"That was Mr. Kane," Mr. G. said as he hung up the phone. "He was very upset about what happened in class today. He wants me to change things in our class. He wants 4A to be like every other classroom."

"You mean with desks and tests and things?" Katie asked him.

Mr. G. nodded.

"No games? Or yoga? Or . . ." Katie continued.

Mr. G. shrugged. "He thinks I haven't done a very good job of controlling you kids. He feels that the kids in 4A have no consideration for other people. You showed that by being so bad when there was a substitute teacher in the class."

Katie frowned. "That's not what we planned at all."

"*Planned?* What are you talking about, Katie?" Mr. G. asked.

Katie kicked at the ground with her toe while she told Mr. G. about how they had all thought he was leaving. And then she explained George's idea for keeping him as their teacher.

"What made you think I was looking for a different job?" Mr. G. asked.

"Well, you cut off your ponytail and then you were absent from school, so Suzanne figured you were probably going on an interview," Katie explained.

"And you listened to *Suzanne*?" Mr. G. asked. "You should have spoken to me. I would have told you that I cut off my ponytail so the hair could be made into a wig."

"A wig?" Katie asked him, surprised.

Mr. G. nodded. "Some kids in this hospital have to take medicine that makes their hair fall out. They need wigs to wear until their real hair grows back. I donated my ponytail to an organization that makes wigs for sick kids."

Katie frowned. "Gosh, Mr. G. That's really nice of you."

Mr. G. sighed. "Well, I guess class 4A is in for some big changes tomorrow," he said slowly.

Katie thought about that. She didn't want to be in a normal classroom with a normal teacher. She wanted everything to be the way it had been up until now. Mr. G. was a great teacher. He made sure the class ran smoothly without being strict or stern. If only there was some way to make Mr. Kane see that.

"Wait!" Katie told Mr. G. excitedly. "I have a great idea!"

Chapter 11

"My sunflower is going to be the first one to pop out of the dirt," George boasted as class 4A headed into their classroom the next morning. "Sunflowers only take a few days to sprout."

"The kids at the hospital will love your sunflowers, George," Katie told him.

"The kids *where* will love my *what*?" George asked, surprised.

"At Cherrydale Children's Hospital," Mr. G. told him. "We're going to donate our plants to the children there. It's all Katie's idea."

"Why would you want to give our plants away?" George demanded of Katie.

"Because *we* see trees and flowers every day," Katie explained. "And the sick kids are stuck inside all the time. We have to be considerate of other people's feelings."

Mr. G. nodded. "That's very important. Mr. Kane thought Katie's idea was very nice."

"It showed him what nice kids we are," Katie told her friends.

"Which was important, since I heard you guys weren't so considerate of Mr. Goodstein's feelings yesterday," Mr. G. added with a sigh. "Okay, everyone sit down now."

Katie grinned as she plopped down in her beanbag chair. No desks for 4A! Her great idea had saved the day! Now things could stay the way they were.

Well, sort of . . .

"I still think you dudes need to brush up on your manners," Mr. G. continued. "This morning, you are each going to write two letters of apology. One to Mr. Goodstein and one to Mr. Kane. And that's just the beginning."

Katie gulped. Uh-oh! Had Mr. G. decided to change things in the class anyway?

"Next week, we're going to have a garden party in our classroom," Mr. G. continued. "We'll drink dandelion tea and have flower-shaped cookies."

"Oh, yeah!" George exclaimed. "Parties rule!"

Mr. G. smiled. "Yes. At our garden party, you will all show perfect manners. That means saying 'please' and 'thank you' and 'excuse me.' There will be no fighting or joke-offs. No one will eat before everyone is served. And no making mushed-up food soup, George."

"That doesn't sound like much of a party," George groaned. "Usually we run around and act silly at parties."

"Oh, I think you did enough of that yesterday," Mr. G. reminded him.

George didn't say another word.

Katie breathed a sigh of relief. Throwing a party to teach manners. How Mr. G. was that?

That night, Katie had a little party of her own. It was a sleepover party for Suzanne and herself. The girls made popcorn, watched movies, and painted each other's fingernails. No surprises. Just a typical sleepover. Until just before Katie's mom came to turn off the lights . . .

"What's that?" Katie asked as Suzanne pulled a pink pouch out of her knapsack.

Suzanne blushed. "N-nothing," she said quickly. "I . . . um . . . I thought your mom was about to turn off the lights."

"Come on. What's in there?" Katie insisted.

Suzanne frowned. "If I show you, you have to promise you won't tell anyone."

"I promise," Katie agreed.

Suzanne held up her little finger. "Pinky swear," she insisted.

Katie crooked her finger through Suzanne's. "Pinky swear."

Suzanne sighed and pulled a thick metal wire out of the bag. It was attached to a cloth band.

"What's that?" Katie asked her.

"My night brace," Suzanne mumbled.

"Your what?" Katie asked, not sure she had heard right.

"My night brace," Suzanne repeated. "I have to wear it on my teeth every night. To make sure they grow in straight."

Katie couldn't believe it! "You've been making fun of Miriam's braces all week," she said. "But you wear them, too?"

"Only at night," Suzanne insisted. "And I hate it. I would never wear anything this ugly if I didn't have to."

"Just like Miriam wouldn't wear braces if she didn't have to," Katie reminded Suzanne.

"At least she gets colored wires," Suzanne said. "I have this plain silver wire with a tan strap. Imagine *me* wearing something bland tan!"

Katie nodded. Now she understood—at least a little—why Suzanne was mean to Miriam. She was jealous that Miriam's braces were prettier than her night brace.

Katie thought for a minute. "Maybe it doesn't have to be so bland," she said finally.

"What are you talking about?" Suzanne asked.

Katie opened her desk drawer and pulled out a package of glitter stickers. "We can decorate the cloth strap with these."

"Hey, that's not a bad idea," Suzanne agreed. "They're glittery. And I'm known for my glitter."

"Exactly," Katie agreed.

"I'll have the funkiest night brace in history," Suzanne said. "It'll be so much cooler than Miriam's red and pink wires."

"Oh, definitely," Katie agreed. She grinned. Suzanne would never change.

But that was okay. In fact, Katie liked that some things stayed the same. She had enough changes in her life. After all, for Katie Kazoo, things changed as often as the wind blew. One, two, switcheroo!

Flowers, Flowers, Everywhere!

Get some flower power of your own. Follow these instructions to make the same paper flowers Mr. G. used to decorate class 4A.

You will need:
Colored tissue paper
Green pipe cleaners
Scissors
A ruler

Here's what you do:
1. Cut tissue paper into 5-inch by 7-inch rectangles.
2. Stack five tissue-paper rectangles. You can use rectangles that are all the same color or different colors.

3. Fold the stack of papers like an accordion.

4. Wrap one end of the pipe cleaner around the middle of the stack of accordion-pleated tissue paper.

5. Gently separate each layer, pulling upward toward the middle of the flower.

6. Make a few flowers and put them in baskets around your house. It will feel like springtime, anytime.